Translated by Christine Prowse
Edited by Virginia Roundell

Published by Marshall Cavendish
Children's Books Limited,
58 Old Compton Street,
London W1V 5PA.

First published by Librairie Hachette
as *Contes de Grimm*
© Hachette, Paris 1978
English translation © Marshall Cavendish Ltd 1980

Printed and bound by
Henri Proost, Turnhout, Belgium.

ISBN 0 85685 842 0

TALES FROM
GRIMM

Adapted by Sybil Capelier

Illustrated by   Michel Guiré-Vaka

The Library of Dreams

John the Faithful

Once upon a time there was an old, old king. This king had a servant who was so devoted to him that he was called John the Faithful. On his death-bed the king left John in charge of his small son.

'My faithful John,' he said. 'You must look after my son as you have looked after me. Only you know the secrets and treasures of my kingdom. Only you can help him. But promise me that he'll never see the portrait of the Princess of the Golden Dome. If he does, he'll be in great danger!'

'Do you think I'm a coward?' cried the young man. 'I shall fight this evil at once! Unlock the door by order of the king!'

The faithful servant had to obey. Sword raised, the young king dashed into the room. But he found no evil: no raven, monster or dragon. Instead, by the gleam of his sword, he saw a beautiful face gazing down at him from an oval frame on the wall.

With a shaking hand he reached out to touch the face and then he fainted. He was carried to his bedchamber where he lay ill for three days. At dawn on the fourth day he awoke.

'I put my trust in you. Goodbye, my faithful John.'
    With these words the old king died. Sadly John made his promise. He put out the candles by the bed and crept from the room.

As the boy grew up, John the Faithful carefully taught him the laws and ways of the land and showed him how to be king. They often explored the palace together from top to bottom. But John kept his promise to the old king: they never stopped at the room with the portrait.
    'You always forget this door, John,' said the prince one morning. 'Open it this time!'
    'No, no, Your Majesty!' shuddered the old servant. 'There's a great evil in that room, blacker than the blackest raven, sharper than a clawed monster and faster than a winged dragon. Come away quickly!'

'Oh, my faithful John; who is the lady in the portrait?' he begged straight away.

'She's the daughter of the King of the Golden Dome,' replied the servant. 'But put her out of your mind, my Lord. You are still weak.'

'I love her,' cried the king. 'And if all the leaves on the trees were tongues they couldn't describe the sweetness of my love. I must marry her or I will die!'

The servant was troubled. He told the king that, in the Kingdom of the Golden Dome, anyone who spoke of love was immediately turned into a tree whose branches grew twisted and bore only dead leaves. The gardens of the King of the Golden Dome were filled with these strange trees.

John the Faithful was in despair but suddenly he had a marvellous idea.

'Then we'll fill a ship with these gifts, disguise ourselves as merchants, and sail off to the land of the Golden Dome. The princess will want to come aboard to see your treasures. We shall weigh anchor then and sail away with her far from that dreadful kingdom!'

This they did and the plan succeeded.

'The princess loves gold,' he said. 'Her goblets and plates and even her buckets and brooms are of solid gold. Tell your goldsmiths to fashion your gold into fine works of art.'

Faithful John had understood the language of the ravens and was afraid for his master. He carefully considered what he would do.

When the ship reached port a magnificent black horse was waiting, prancing and snorting with impatience. Before the king could mount the horse, John leapt forward and slew the animal in an instant. There were cries of horror from the courtiers.

'Let him be!' cried the king. 'He is John the Faithful and I trust him!'

Arriving at the palace, the king was presented with a sparkling silver wedding robe on a golden tray. But, as he reached for it, his servant threw him aside, snatched the robe and flung it into the fire.

The princess loved gold so much that she seemed blind to everything else. She laughed with delight at the birds, bowls, beads and other beautiful gifts of pure gold which the prince showed her. While she was busy admiring them all, the handsome king slipped off his merchant's cloak and the princess saw who he really was.

'When I saw your portrait I fainted right to the ground,' he said.

At first the princess was afraid, but the king was so young and handsome that she soon fell in love with him.

Before long the king's ship was sailing far out on the open sea. John the Faithful was standing on the deck when three ravens landed near him.

'Hark, hark!' said the first. 'We've found the Princess of the Golden Dome!'

'She'll be dead within a week!' said the second.

'And so will the prince!' added the third. 'He'll see a horse as black as the night. He'll climb on its back and be carried forever around the heavens!'

'Or else,' said the second, 'he'll put on his wedding robe and disappear in a puff of smoke and flame!'

'The princess will die within a week!' repeated the first raven. 'She'll receive three drops of poisoned blood. Anyone who tries to save her will be turned to stone!'

Then they all flew off into the distance, crying, 'Hark, hark, hark!'

'Well?' demanded the king.

John told him all about the three ravens. As he spoke the last word of his story John the Faithful turned to stone, but the young queen returned to life.

The king and the queen wept bitter tears. They had the statue of the faithful servant placed in their bedchamber. Whenever they looked at it they wept and cried, 'Oh, forgive us, Faithful John! How little we rewarded your loyalty!'

Some time later the queen gave birth to twin sons. They were a constant joy to her and the king. One day, while she was in church, the king was passing John's statue and cried out, 'Is there nothing I can do to bring you back to life?'

To his amazement, the statue replied, 'Certainly there is, if you are willing to sacrifice your children, as I sacrificed myself for you.'

With a heavy heart, the king did as the statue asked. He went home and cut off the heads of his two children. Instantly John sprang to life before him.

At that moment the queen returned and, seeing the bodies of her sons, fainted with grief. But John the Faithful took the two heads, set them on the boys' shoulders and the twins came back to life. The queen recovered and they all lived happily together for the rest of their lives.

By now the courtiers were all grumbling and whispering about John.

'Let him be!' cried the king. 'He is John the Faithful and I trust him!'

The wedding celebrations then began with a great feast and ball. During the third dance the beautiful bride grew pale and sank to the floor in a dead faint. On her shoulder were three drops of scarlet blood. Once again John leapt forward. This time he sucked the deadly poison and spat it out.

But, at this, the king became jealous.

'Throw him into prison!' he cried.

'Let me speak first, Your Majesty,' begged Faithful John.

The Seven Worthies

One day seven worthy gentlemen were seated around a café table in a small town. There was a tall one, a fat one, a sly one, a jolly one, a gruff one and, last of all, Septimus, the silliest one. Their leader was Mugwump, the town mayor.

Through the thick smoke of their pipes, seven little glasses were raised and the cry could be heard, 'Long live the Society of the Seven Globe-trotters!' For they had decided to travel the world together in search of daring deeds and great adventure.

These seven respectable gentlemen talked far into the night. They plotted and planned and dreamed and schemed of all they would do and see:

'We shall fight the mightiest monster!'
'And win the greatest battle!'
'And ford the fastest river!'

Early next morning they all lined up outside Mugwump's house, ready to set off.

Septimus, the silliest one, had made them a spear: a single spear, but so long and so heavy that all seven would have to carry it!

Mugwump, the mayor, would go first, of course, as he was the bravest and boldest of them all. The others would follow in order of age, right down to Septimus, who was the youngest.

And so off they set, cheered by all the people of the town.

Now, one day, while they were tramping cheerfully along a quiet country lane, leaning sleepily on their spear, an insect flew out from behind them.

It was only some bug or beetle, buzzing about its business. But the seven worthies thought it was an attack. Dropping their spear on the spot, they all dived head first over the nearest bushes and buried themselves deep in the grass.

Suddenly, Mugwump gave forth a cry. He had dived last, as he was the bravest and boldest, and had landed fair and square on the prongs of an old farm rake. Up came the handle and felled him with one blow!

'Aaah! Oooh! Eeeh!' he howled. 'I surrender!'

'If you surrender, so do we!' cried the other six, popping up one after the other. 'We are your prisoners!'

There was no answer since the only enemy was a harmless insect. Feeling rather relieved but also shamefaced, they hastened on, agreeing among themselves to forget the little adventure.

The second danger they met was quite different. The next day they were marching, single file as usual, across a misty moor. Mugwump saw the dreadful monster first as he was in the lead.

This wild and terrible animal was nothing more than a hare. But the seven worthies knew they had to be on guard against everything. They hid behind a hazel tree and discussed what to do.

'We must rush to the attack!' decided the mayor. 'Boldness and surprise will be our strongest weapons!'
'We will fight to the last man!' cried Septimus, the last man.

So they set off into battle against the monster.

Mugwump, the mayor, was in the lead, of course, as he was the bravest and boldest. But he did not seem to be in much of a hurry.

Septimus remembered the shame of their last adventure and cried from the end of the line:
'Forward with the spear, my friends;
Here's our chance to make amends!'
The next one took up the cry:
'We'll cross the meadow into war –
This hairy beast will be no more!'
The jolly one joined in:
'In this great battle we'll find fame
And illustrious will be our name!'

The poor mayor, urged on by these heroic outbursts, broke into a puffing, panting run.

The nearer he drew to the foe the greater the mayor's terror grew. Finally, a loud wail burst from his lips: 'Eeehow! Eeehow! Eeehow!'
At this, the hare woke up and took flight. Mugwump stopped dead. His six followers collapsed behind him in a higgledy-piggledy heap.
Joyfully the mayor cried:
'My six brave men: look there, look there!
The dreadful monster was a hare!'
With this the second adventure came to an end.

The seven globe-trotters continued on their way, up hill and down dale in search of further fame and fortune.

At last, after many days march, they reached the banks of a great river. Never had they seen a river so deep and so green.

They sat in silence, gazing in wonder at its waters.

Far on the other bank a farmer saw them sitting thus. He thought they had lost something in the water and cried out, 'What have you lost? What have you lost?'

Mugwump thought he was saying, 'Why don't you cross? Why don't you cross?' Being the bravest and boldest, he plunged into the water and was quickly carried away downstream by the current.

Only his hat reached the other side.

Here it was pounced upon by a big, fat frog. Delighted by his discovery, he sat on the hat and sang, 'Croak, croak!'

'I can hear our leader calling us,' said Septimus. 'I think he's saying, "Cross, cross!"'

Seizing their spear, they all jumped, feet first, into the mighty stream. In an instant, they too floated away down the river.

Whether any of them ever reached home again I don't know. If they did, they never boasted of their adventures.

Rapunzel

Once upon a time there was a young woman who was expecting a baby. She was very happy as she had long wished for a child.

Behind this woman's house there was a garden surrounded by a high stone wall. It was a beautiful garden, full of delicious fruit and vegetables. However, the garden belonged to a wicked old witch and no one dared enter it.

One hot summer's day the young woman opened her bedroom window to enjoy the breeze which blew from the hills.

As she was standing gazing over the witch's garden her eye fell upon a bed of radishes. They were such magnificent vegetables: plump and crisp and appetizing.

The young woman longed to make a salad of them. Every day she returned to the window and her longing became so great that she could think of nothing else. She did not tell her husband for fear that he would enter the witch's garden. Finally, however, she fell ill with longing.

'What is it you want, my dear wife?' begged her husband, who was afraid she would die.

But she would not tell him.

As the days passed by she grew paler and weaker. At last, in despair, she whispered, 'The radishes in the witch's garden! I must have them or I will surely die!'

The man loved his wife dearly. So, that night, by the light of the moon, he climbed swiftly over the witch's wall.

He did not see the witch standing in the corner of the garden. He filled his bag with radishes and was about to run off when a shrill voice broke the silence of the night.

'That will cost you dearly, young man!'

'Oh, d-dear witch!' stammered the husband. 'Be m-merciful. My wife is dying and only your radishes will save her!'

'Take what you will!' cackled the witch. 'But, in exchange, you must give me your child when it is born!'

In his terror, the poor man agreed to the witch's demand.

He returned home and prepared the salad for his wife. The colour returned to her cheeks. She smiled again and the witch was soon forgotten.

However, a few months later a beautiful baby girl was born. And, very soon, the witch appeared by the cradle.

'I'll call her Rapunzel!' she cackled as she carried the baby off.

Time passed. The little girl's hair grew and grew, shining as brilliantly as the sun and silky soft. By the time she was twelve years old it fell to her feet like a golden waterfall.

The old witch became very jealous of Rapunzel's beauty. So, she took her into the forest one day and locked her in a tall tower. This tower had no door and no stairs: only a tiny window at the very top.

When she came to see the child, the witch would cry:

'Rapunzel, Rapunzel,
Let down your hair!'

The little girl would let her silken braid fall to the foot of the tower. The old witch would climb slowly up to the window.

Years went by. Rapunzel passed the lonely hours brushing her golden tresses and sweetly singing the songs the witch had taught her.

One day the king's son was out riding in the forest. He heard Rapunzel's beautiful voice floating down from the tower. He stopped to listen, thinking that surely he must be dreaming for it was lovelier than anything he had ever heard.

The prince went all around the walls of the tower but could find no way in. He was about to ride off when he heard a crackle of leaves on the ground. There stood the witch, calling:
'Rapunzel, Rapunzel,
Let down your hair!'
The king's son watched, hidden from view, as the young girl let down her braid and the witch climbed up.

When the witch had left, the prince went to the tower and called:
'Rapunzel, Rapunzel,
Let down your hair!'
Down came the braid and the prince climbed up the tower, just as the witch had done.

Rapunzel was greatly alarmed when she saw a stranger at her window. But the prince spoke kindly to her and soon she lost her fear.

Every day he returned to see her and before long they fell in love.

Of course, the wicked old witch knew nothing of the prince's visits until, one day, Rapunzel said thoughtlessly, 'Oh, why are you so slow to climb, old witch! The prince is much quicker than you!'

Seizing Rapunzel's hair in one hand and a pair of scissors in the other, she cut off the girl's long golden tresses.

Then she took the poor girl far away to a desert land and there she left her all alone.

The next day the prince returned to the tower and called:

'Rapunzel, Rapunzel,
Let down your hair!'

The crafty witch hung down the braid of hair that she had cut off. Just as the prince reached the window and saw her angry face, she let the braid go. The poor young man went tumbling down into the brambles at the foot of the tower. His eyes pierced by thorns, he stumbled off, blind and miserable, in search of his beloved.

And so he wandered, until he came at last to the desert. Here he heard someone weeping. Through the tears he recognized the voice of poor Rapunzel.

When the young girl saw the prince she fell into his arms and wept. Two tears fell into the prince's eyes and, in an instant, he could see again.

They returned together to the prince's kingdom where they were married and lived happily till the end of their days.

The witch's fury was frightful.

'How dare you deceive me!' she shrieked.

The Wren and the Bear

'That's the king of the birds,' replied the wolf with a grin. 'He is the greatest bird of all. You should bow down to him!'

One evening a bear and a wolf sat chatting in the forest. Above their heads a nestful of wrens were singing in the trunk of an old oak tree.

'Tell me, my learned friend,' said the bear. 'Who dares to deafen us with such a terrible racket?'

'If he is a king, he must have a castle,' said the bear. 'For a king without a castle cannot be very great!'

The wolf tried to hide his smile, wondering how long the joke would last.
'But he does have a castle, my dear bear,' said the wolf. 'And you shall see it for yourself. But we must wait till the king and queen have flown off tomorrow morning.'

The bear had never seen a royal castle. He grew very excited and stomped and growled all night. At last dawn came and the king and queen left their nest. The bear and the wolf crept back to the tree.

The bear pushed his nose into the old tree trunk.
'A royal castle indeed!' he cried. 'This isn't a royal castle! It's not even a house! It's more like a cottage! And these cheeky little chicks . . . you can't call them princes!'

The baby wrens were most indignant to hear the bear speak of them so.

They let forth such a wail of protest that the bear and the wolf quickly fled in fright.

'That bear insulted us!' shrieked the little wrens when their parents returned. 'We won't eat a single worm till you have taught him a lesson!'

'So be it!' cried the father. And off he flew to peck angrily at the bear's door.

'You've insulted my children!' he squawked. 'It's war, you old growler! War from now on!'

So all the four-footed animals of the forest came together for the fray. And every bird and bee and every other flying creature gathered near the wren's nest.

But, into the bear's camp there came a spy. This spy was a gnat and this is what he overheard:

'You are the craftiest of all, old fox,' growled the bear. 'So you shall lead us into battle. But how will you signal us?'

'With my fine, bushy, red tail,' replied the fox, proudly turning around so that all could see it. 'As long as it is raised, fight on. But as soon as it falls, run for your lives.'

The gnat flew straight back to the wren and told him of the fox's plan.

Then the battle began!

The earth trembled and shook beneath the thundering charge of the four-footed animals. The sky buzzed to the beating of wings as the wren and his friends flew to the attack.

The Wren and the Bear

Closer and closer the two armies drew till they met with a crash and a roar and a squawking and shrieking. And, throughout it all, the red, red tail of the fox stood like a flag.

But the clever wren had sent a hornet to sit under the fox's tail.

With the first sting, the fox gave a mighty yell. But his tail stayed upright. With the second sting, he gave a mighty leap. The other beasts fought harder, thinking the fox was battling fiercely. Still the tail stood upright. With the third sting, down came the tail, up went a howl and off sped the fox as fast as his legs could carry him.

With that, all his followers turned tail too and fled, helter-skelter, back to their homes.

And that is how, with a trick, the wren came to be king of the battlefield.

The king and the queen returned home where they found their little ones very hungry indeed. They all sat down to a feast of worms and rejoiced that the bear had been taught to mind his manners.

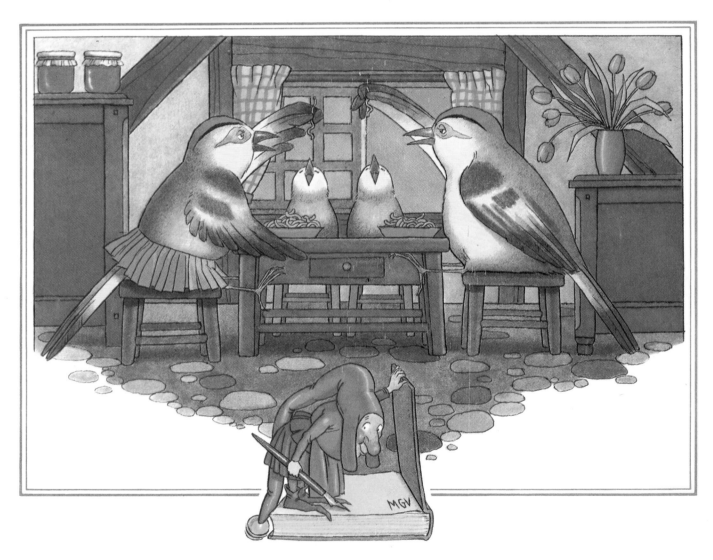

PRINTED IN BELGIUM BY
proost
INTERNATIONAL BOOK PRODUCTION

PRINTED IN BELGIUM BY
proost
INTERNATIONAL BOOK PRODUCTION